Conte

Rosa   Jules

CHAPTER 1

It's On!

Rosa runs across the school
playground towards her best friend,
Jules, who is sitting under a tree
eating her lunch.

Rosa "Jules! Hey, look over there! It's finally up!"

Jules "What's up?"

Rosa "The notice about the school play. Come on!"

Rosa rushes back to the main school building with Jules only a few steps behind. The girls run over to a noticeboard that's outside the staff room. The notice reads:

This year's school play auditions will be held at lunchtime tomorrow in Mr. Tuttle's classroom.

Rosa "Great, the audition is with
Mr. Tuttle. He's pretty cool so this
year's play should be something
special, I reckon. What are you going
to do for your audition, Jules?"

Jules "Um, I don't know. I get really
nervous with all that stuff."

Rosa "Yes, me too, but it'll be really cool once we get into it!"

Jules "I suppose so. I'd really like an acting part but I just can't sing that well. I sound more like a goose with a bad cold."

Rosa "No, you don't. And anyway, no-one says you have to sing. We don't even know yet if there's music in it."

Jules "Oh, OK then. I can always be a tree and wave my lovely leaves around silently—boring!"

Rosa "It'll be fine—you'll see. This will be the best school play ever!"

CHAPTER 2

The Audition

Rosa and Jules are waiting with
some other children outside
Mr. Tuttle's classroom. After a
few minutes Mr. Tuttle lets everyone
in. He asks them to sit down and
to wait for him to call them.

Rosa "I feel really nervous now. But I think it's normal to feel like that. Some actors say it even helps them perform better."

Jules "I once heard that a boy from Sommerville School was so nervous when he walked out on stage that he wet himself. He was dressed as a pineapple and he had this huge stain that everyone could see."

Rosa giggles.

Jules "Imagine if that happened to me—I'd just die!"

Rosa "Yes, I reckon it would be *so* embarrassing, but it won't happen. We'll be OK. This is our big chance to be school play stars. If we're really worried, we can just think of the headteacher doing something really stupid. We'll soon forget all about being scared."

Jules "Yes! Thanks, I'll keep that in mind. What do you think Mr. Tuttle will make us do?"

Rosa "Well, we might have to read something or pretend we're something weird. Or maybe he'll get us to do some dance moves or to sing a bit."

Jules "Sing? I don't think so!"

Rosa "Well, I don't know. I'm just saying we might have to try different things, that's all."

Jules "Maybe this isn't such a good idea—I don't feel so good."

Rosa "Don't be silly! You'll be all right. You never know what might happen. Look, It's our turn next. Mr. Tuttle is waving us in."

Jules "Oh, no. I'm desperate. I need to go really bad."

Rosa "Too late for that. Just hold on. We're in this together, remember."

CHAPTER 3

Hip-hop Porridge

The next day, Mr. Tuttle tells Jules and Rosa they have both been chosen for the school play. He tells them that the play will be "The Three Bears", hip-hop style.

Jules "I just can't believe I got the lead role. My singing must have been OK after all. I hope I make a cool Goldilocks. I think I'll wear a wig so I'll look like Kylie. What do you think? Rosa? What's up?"

Rosa "Nothing."

Jules "Are you sure?"

Rosa "How come you get the main part and all I get to be is a dumb bowl of porridge? You didn't even want to audition in the first place."

Jules "Yes, but you won't be just any bowl of porridge. You'll be the one that's 'not too hot, not too cold, but just right'. And from what Mr. Tuttle says, you'll be the best hip-hopping bowl of porridge ever!"

Rosa "Yes, well it's still not as good as Goldilocks."

Jules "If you're that worried I can ask Mr. Tuttle to swap us. I'm still scared that I might lose it in front of the audience. How would that be? They'd call me "Goldilost" instead of Goldilocks!"

Rosa "Thanks for the offer, Jules,
but I'll stick with my porridge.
You'll be great as Goldilocks."

Jules suddenly has a thought.

Jules "Wait here, I've got an idea."

Before Rosa can say anything, Jules races across the playground towards the staff room.

CHAPTER 4

Undercover Acting

A few minutes later, Jules returns to where Rosa is sitting in the playground.

Jules "I asked Mr. Tuttle if you can learn everyone else's parts, just in case someone gets sick and can't appear, on the night. He thinks it's a great idea and said you should come to the practice. Please, please, please do it!"

Rosa "OK then."

Jules "Cool! Mr. Tuttle wants us to write our own hip-hop lyrics, so we can write the words for Goldilocks together—you'll be much better at it than me."

Rosa "And he said I can learn all the main parts, right? Mummy, Daddy and Baby Bear, your part and the chairs?"

Jules "Yes!"

Rosa "Cool! Imagine if someone really does get sick on the night and can't do it. But it probably won't happen. Everyone wants to be in the play too much. They'd be dying and still go on!"

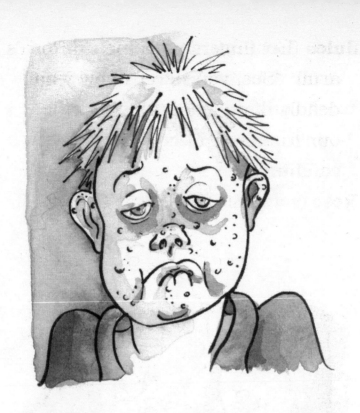

Jules "Well, you never know. Billy Cooper is always getting sick. Remember when he came to school with huge red spots all over his face?"

Rosa "Oh yes, that was totally gross! He had like a million spots all over him."

Jules (her fingers creeping up Rosa's arm) "See, you never know what deadly disease is lurking inside our friends, and might be catching!"

Rosa (screaming) "Oh, no! Get lost!"

CHAPTER 5

The Big Night

It's Friday night and the parents and friends are all moving into their seats in the school hall.

Backstage, teachers are calling out, "Next for make-up! Jamie to wardrobe!" Jules, dressed in her Goldilocks hip-hop clothing, can see Rosa in her bowl of porridge outfit. Suddenly Mr. Tuttle appears and whispers something in Rosa's ear.

Jules "What's going on, Rosa?"

Rosa "You're not going to believe it! Rebecca Allan's mother just phoned to say Rebecca's got a tummy bug and can't get out of bed and Mr. Tuttle wants me to play her part—Daddy Bear!"

Jules "That's brilliant! I mean, bad for Rebecca but really cool for you."

Rosa "Mr. Tuttle said when I've done my bowl of porridge scene I have to quickly dress as Daddy Bear and be ready for his 'grunting groaning' act."

Jules "Great! That's my favourite part of the whole show and now you're doing it!"

Rosa "But what about all the people out there? What if I mess up the beat? I hope I'm ready."

Jules "If you get nervous just do what we said."

Rosa "What do you mean?"

Jules "You know, just imagine the
  headteacher doing something
  dumb!"
Rosa "Oh yes, that's right."

Rosa takes a peek through the
curtains and looks out at the
audience, all waiting. She feels a
wave of excitement come over her.

Rosa (turning back to Jules) "Hey Jules, it's time. Break a leg!"
Jules "You too. Good luck!"

As the lights dim, hip-hop music starts booming through the school hall. All the actors take their places with Jules centre stage. Then on with the show! Before they know it, it's time to take a bow.

Jules (whispering to Rosa) You know
   Rosa, I wouldn't have been
   Goldilocks if it wasn't for you.
   We're both school play stars now!"
Rosa "You bet!"

After three encores, the curtain
falls as the audience claps loudly for
the last time. Everyone agrees that
the kids have been great—definite
stars in the making!

Jules

GIRLS ROCK!
School Play Lingo

Rosa

break a leg An expression said to an actor before they go on stage to wish them good luck for their performance. It doesn't mean that they should fall off their skateboard and break their leg!

curtain call When an actor comes out on stage, through the closed curtains, at the end of a performance.

encore A French word that means "again". People shout it out at a live performance because they want to see or hear the performer on stage one more time.

stage manager Someone who is in charge of what happens on the stage. They talk quietly to the backstage crew through their headsets.

GIRLS ROCK!

School Play Must-dos

☆ Make sure that you know your lines—it's embarrassing when you're on stage with nothing to say!

☆ Don't forget to put your stage make-up on so that you look even more beautiful than normal.

☆ Make sure you do your costume up properly. How bad would it be if it fell off while you were on stage!

☆ Have fun—that's what it's all about!

☆ Tell all your friends, family and relatives that you are in a play. At least then there will be someone there to watch you and cheer at the end.

☆ If you have to kiss a boy during an acting scene, make sure you wash your lips afterwards to get rid of all the boy germs—Boys R Yuk!

☆ Learn to sign your name really well—you never know how many autographs you'll need to sign in the years to come.

☆ Practise making faces in a mirror so you look like different people. It's sort of like taking on different roles in a play. But make sure your brother doesn't see you—he'll never let you forget it!

GIRLS ROCK!

School Play
Instant Info

🌙 William Shakespeare wrote many plays that theatre companies and schools all over the world still perform.

🌙 In big theatres, the stage manager sits in the left corner of the stage (where the audience can't see them). That corner is often called the "prompt corner".

🌙 The prompt corner get its name from the olden days. If an actor on stage forgot what to say, someone would call out lines from the corner of the stage in a loud whisper.

🌙 Katherine Hepburn has won more Oscars in the American Academy Awards than any other actor.

🌙 The oldest indoor theatre in the world is in Vicenza, Italy. It was built in the late 1580s and still survives in its original form.

🌙 Mary-Kate and Ashley Olsen are the highest paid child actors in the world. The sale of all their books, hats, bags, videos and everything else earns them around $0.5 billion each year.

Think Tank

1 Who wears headsets on the stage?

2 When someone has butterflies in their stomach what does that mean?

3 Costumes are the special clothes actors wear in a play. True or false?

4 What does a make-up artist do?

5 "Rehearse" is another word for what? (It begins with the letter p.)

6 A make-up artist makes up stories. True or false?

7 Is William Shakespeare a singer?

8 How many people would be in a one-man play?

Answers

8 There is one person in a one-man play, of course, but it's not always a man!

7 No, he wrote many plays long ago that are still performed today.

6 False. A make-up artist puts make-up on actors.

5 "Rehearse" is another word for "practise".

4 A make-up artist puts make-up on the actors and dancers before the show.

3 It's true that costumes are the special clothes actors wear.

2 To have butterflies means that you're nervous. Professional actors always say it's good to have a few butterflies as it helps you perform better.

1 Stage managers wear headsets so that they can talk to the backstage crew and hear their replies.

How did you score?

- If you got 8 answers correct, then look out—a star is born! You love the theatre and sometimes dream of a career in show business!

- If you got 6 answers correct, you like acting and with hard work you might be able to star in a school play.

- If you got fewer than 4 answers correct, you probably prefer watching plays to starring in them.

Hey Girls!

I have loads of fun reading books and plays. Sometimes I imagine I'm really acting at a big theatre, and if I close my eyes I can see what the setting and costumes look like.

I don't have a favourite play but I think it would be really good fun to sing and dance! My family and friends could be in the front row and they could all clap at the end of the show I'm in!

You can make reading fun too by acting out the stories you read. Here are some ideas for making "School Play Stars" fun to read.

Find some costumes (or make some) for Goldilocks and the rapping bowl of porridge.

Use chairs as props and choose some good background music. So ... have you decided who is going to be Rosa and who is going to be Jules? And what about the narrator?

Now act out the story in front of your friends—I'm sure you'll all have a great time! You also might like to take this story home and get someone in your family to read it with you. Maybe they can take on a part in the story.

Books are like adventures, you just don't know where the next one will take you! So make sure you have fun reading.

And remember, Girls Rock!

Julie

GIRLS ROCK!
When We Were Kids

Julie

Holly

Julie talked with Holly, another *Girls Rock!* author.

Julie "Were you ever in a school play, Holly? My favourite part was Maria in 'The Sound of Music'."

Holly "Yes, I was in 'The Wizard of Oz' as Dorothy."

Julie "Imagine if we did a play together. I'd be Maria and you'd be Dorothy."

Holly "Yes, and we could call it 'The Wizard of Music'."

Julie "Or 'The Sound of Oz'!"

Holly "Or I know … 'The Girls from Oz' starring Julie and Holly."

Julie "Now you're talking (or more like singing?). That's my kind of play!"

GIRLS ROCK!
What a Laugh!

Q What did the stage manager say to the actor?

A If you were any more wooden, we'd have to move you around with the furniture.

GIRLS ROCK!

Read about the fun
that girls have in these
GIRLS ROCK! titles:

The Sleepover

Pool Pals

Bowling Buddies

Girl Pirates

Netball Showdown

School Play Stars

Diary Disaster

Horsing Around

GIRLS ROCK! books are available from
most booksellers. For mail order information
please call Rising Stars on 01933 443862 or visit
www.risingstars-uk.com